. . . And Then the Feather Fell

...And Then the Feather Fell

Wade Blevins

Illustrated by
Wade Blevins

Ozark Publishing, Inc.
P.O. Box 228
Prairie Grove, AR 72753

Library of Congress Cataloging-in-Publication Data

Blevins, Wade, 1973-
    And then the feather fell / Wade Blevins ; illustrated
by Wade Blevins.
        p. cm. — (The Cherokee Indian legend series ; 1)
        Summary: Laura, a Cherokee girl who lives with
her beloved grandmother, faces the reality of an old legend
about the owl when her grandmother becomes ill.
        ISBN 1-56763-096-0 (cloth : alk. paper). — ISBN
1-56763-097-9 (pbk. : alk. paper)
        1. Cherokee Indians—Juvenile fiction. 2. Youths'
writings, American. [1. Cherokee Indians—Fiction. 2.
Indians of North America—Fiction. 3. Grandmothers —
Fiction. 4. Youths' writings.]
        I. Title. II Series: Blevins, Wade, 1973-
Cherokee Indian legend series. : 1.
        PZ7.B61865An   1996
        [Fic}—dc20
        96-10304
        CIP
        AC

Ozark Publishing, Inc.
P.O. Box 228
Prairie Grove, AR 72753
Ph: 1-800-321-5671

Printed in the United States of America

ACKNOWLEDGMENT

I would like to thank my 103-year-old great-grandmother, who passed on her knowledge of the past to present and future generations and, in so doing, helped to preserve our Cherokee culture. Maude Parris Gardner, born of a Cherokee father and an English mother, was raised on the Illinois River in Indian Territory, now Oklahoma. Her stories of Cherokee superstitions and her knowledge of wild herbs and plants to be used as medicine and food have provided the family with hours of entertainment. In this age where everyone is attempting to find his or her identity, through her I know who I truly am. Through the efforts of Native Americans, our culture will remain for our children and our children's children. It is not the color of one's skin, but the content of our heart that denotes a true *Aniyunwiya*, a Cherokee. *Wa Do* (Thank You).

FOREWORD

A little girl's love for her grandmother and her knowledge of the legend of the owl feather causes her much grief and concern.

. . . And Then the Feather Fell

Other books in this series

Path of Destiny

Legend of Little Deer

Ganseti and the Legend of the Little People

The Wisdom Circle

Atagahi's Gift

Selu's Song

Silver mists curled around the jagged peaks and gnarled cedars of the Smokey Mountains. These giant peaks that dominated the Carolinas were home to Laura and her grandmother, Elisi Rainmaker.

They lived peacefully with the rest
of their Cherokee family, the Wolf
Clan.

Small cabins nestled in the huge valley that had been their protector for countless generations. The cabins fanned out from the seven-sided Council House like willow shoots.

The sun was casting its last rays on the tips of the mountain peaks as Laura made her way to

Grandmother's small, one-room cabin that they both shared.

Laura was a small child when smallpox, or the "Intruder," as the Cherokees said, took her mother and father and older brother. Laura had no recollection of her parents or her brother and had always thought of Grandmother Rainmaker as both father and mother.

Laura's moccasined feet made little noise as she entered the cabin, but Grandmother heard her and looked up and smiled. She motioned for Laura to climb onto her lap so they could share their favorite time of day. The work was done, and they could sit together near the fire, and Grandmother would tell her stories. Grandmother Rainmaker was the best storyteller in the entire village.

"What story will you tell today, Grandmother?"

Grandmother's wizened eyes gazed out into the distance as she lovingly stroked the long, raven-colored hair of her granddaughter. Softly, she began to speak.

"This is what my grandmother told me when I was a little girl," she began, settling Laura more comfortably into the folds of her bright cotton tear dress and apron. Laura looked into her grandmother's face and thought that her words were

slower and the wrinkles around her eyes were deeper than before.

"A long time ago, when the earth was still young and all the animals could speak the same language, there lived the 'Father of Owls.' He lived in an old, lightning-struck tree at the very edge of the great forest. Now this owl was very

evil and would eat the livers of all the other animals. They were very afraid of Father Owl, so they all met

in secret one day for a council, trying to decide what must be done to save themselves.

"The animal council came to a decision. They would cast a spell on the owl, making him hunt only during the night and sleep during the day. 'So be it!'

"When Father Owl discovered

that he had been cursed, he became
enraged and flew to the council. He
landed in the very center of the

meeting and called out in a voice
like thunder, 'Since my curse can-
not be undone, I will curse you.
From this day on, when you find a
feather off my coat on a bush or a
tree, *beware*, for someone will fall

deathly ill. The feather must stay on the bush for four days or that person will die.' And with a mighty flap of his wings, he disappeared into the night, making good his curse. And so it is with all of his descendants today."

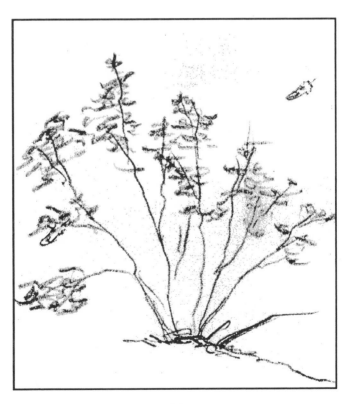

Elisi Rainmaker sat quietly for a few minutes, then she looked down at Laura and smiled sadly. Laura had fallen asleep.

When Laura opened her eyes the next morning, the sun was already peeking over the mountains. She rubbed the sleep from her eyes and got up to help her grandmother with breakfast. Grandmother was still on her pallet, deathly pale beneath her coffee-colored skin. Her faded eyes were

weak and no longer held the exuberant sparkle that they had the night before. Laura put a hand to her forehead and found it burning hot to the touch. Grandmother's eyes closed, and her breath rattled unevenly in her throat.

Frantically, Laura rushed outside to fix her grandmother a healing tea. She began collecting the herbs in the bright Smokey Mountain sunlight. Laura bent to pick some Spicewood for the tea

and noticed a small object fluttering in the wind. Laura gasped as she realized that it was an owl feather that was caught in the Spicewood bush. It danced in the breeze, hanging by a few of the downy hairs near the base of the feather. Surely the feather would fall before the sun went down behind the mountains.

Laura knew the feather could not possibly stay in the bush for four more days. She reached up and clutched a fistful of her hair and yanked as hard as she could. Tears came to her eyes, but she kept

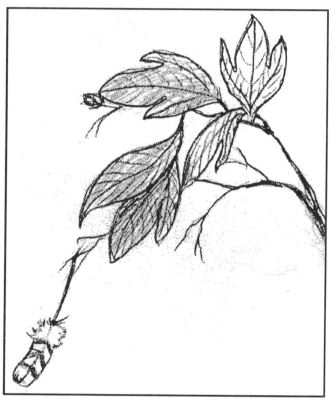

pulling until she had several strands of hair, which she braided into a crude string. This she tied to the feather; then she tied the other end to the Spicewood bush, hoping it would remain for four days.

Each day Laura got up early and rushed to check the feather, keeping watch all day and only leaving to give her grandmother some healing tea.

The tea did no good, however, and Elisi Rainmaker grew weaker and more pale.

Laura prayed each day for her grandmother to be spared. For three days she kept her vigil, hope growing with the setting of each sun.

On the fourth day, a terrible storm hit, darkening the sky until it looked like night. As the lightning flashed, Laura stayed near her grandmother, hugging her tightly.

Laura got up late in the afternoon to look out the doorway. In the flashes of lightning she could see the feather

whipping in the winds, straining at the hair string. Laura rushed outside

to tie the string better, when suddenly
a clap of thunder and a spear of lightning arrowed down, obliterating the

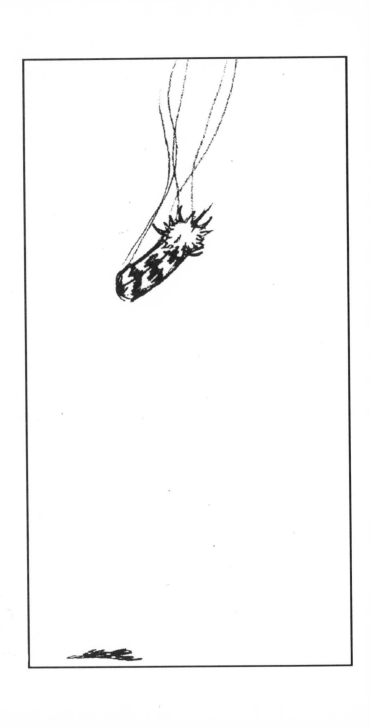

small Spicewood bush. Laura watched as the feather was pitched high in the air, dancing wildly with the sparks from the fire.

... and then the feather fell.

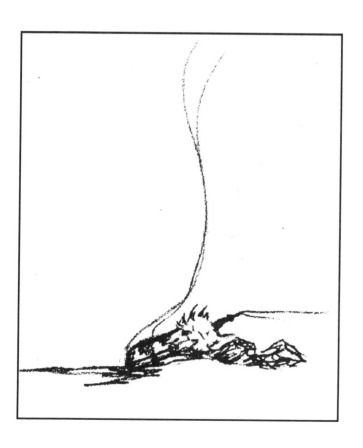

EDIBLE WILD PLANTS

A favorite food of the Cherokee is wild onions. The long, slender leaves and onion-like bulbs are found growing along streamside woodlands. Wild onions are considered delicious when fried in bacon grease with scrambled eggs. Also, the Cherokees crushed the leaves of the wild onion and rubbed them over their bodies as an insect repellent.

REMEDY

Seven flowers taken from the "jewel-weed" and rubbed over the skin will cure poison ivy.

SUPERSTITION

If a bluejay feather is found by chance on the ground, rubbing it across a baby's lips will make the child an early riser.